D1049953

A PIG, A FOX, AND A FOX

For teachers, past and present,
with gratefulness and admiration—JF

PENGUIN WORKSHOP
An Imprint of Penguin Random House LLC, New York

Copyright © 2020 by Jonathan Fenske. All rights reserved. Published by Penguin Workshop, an imprint of Penguin Random House LLC, New York. PENGUIN and PENGUIN WORKSHOP are trademarks of Penguin Books Ltd, and the W colophon is a registered trademark of Penguin Random House LLC. Manufactured in China.

Visit us online at www.penguinrandomhouse.com.

Library of Congress Cataloging-in-Publication Data is available.

ISBN 9781524792121 (paperback)   10 9 8 7 6 5 4 3 2 1
ISBN 9780593382561 (library binding)   10 9 8 7 6 5 4 3 2 1

A PIG, A FOX, AND A FOX

by Jonathan Fenske

Penguin Workshop

PART ONE

5

I look around.
Where is that Fox?

Tee-hee.

I see a wall.
A wall of blocks.

11

I bumped the wall.
The wall of blocks.

The wall will fall!
And so will Fox!

I will catch you!
Do not fear!

Your good friend Pig
is always here!

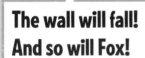

PLOP!

16

You silly Pig! That was a doll.

That was not Fox up on the wall!

I saved a doll.

I bumped some blocks.

I smashed a wall.

PART TWO

Pig has a house.

Pig has a door.

I knock and knock.

KNOCK! KNOCK!

KNOCK!

I knock some more.

One Fox will hide.
One Fox will stay.

Two foxes will
trick Pig today.

22

23

Groan.

You are not Fox.
You are his doll.

24

I heard some knocks.

KNOCK!
KNOCK!
KNOCK!

CLICK.

I turned the locks.

CLICK.

I broke a door.

CRACK!

27

PART THREE

But we have had enough today.

31

32